THE NEIGHBOR

THE NEIGHBOR

Straight Men Book 1: Jeff & Danny

S.H. AZANON

BOHEME PRESS

THE
NEIGHBOR

1

JEFF

PEOPLE SAY DIVORCE is just another name for freedom, and I got to test that theory first-hand. The wife—correction, *ex*-wife—moved to Rhode Island with her girlfriend (now her fiance) almost six months ago; the kids were at college in Massachusetts; and our suburban Stamford home in Connecticut was now my private little kingdom. I got to eat whatever I wanted, be as loud as I wanted, have sex with whomever I choose. I could walk around naked —okay, yeah, I was doing that before too, but now there was no one nagging me about it.

("Put some clothes on, Jeff, for God's sake!" I could still hear my ex's voice in my head. "The boys are around, they could see you!" Yeah, like their heads would explode if they saw their dad's dong, for crying out loud. They had them too, almost the exact replicas of mine. But no, as long as she was around, the underwear had to stay on too. I thought maybe she was bothered by my size; I knew my dick was extra large and it made sex uncomfortable for her. Didn't realize at the time that she was just not that into cock.)

Well, I was sure making up for lost time now: I slept naked, and in the morning when I woke up hard and throbbing, I went naked to the bathroom, beat my meat in the shower, then put on some comfy T-shirt and stayed bottomless for the rest of the day. The summer was in full swing, and since I mostly worked from home these days, that was my standard attire. If there was some unexpected business emergency, or a call from a client, I was still presentable, none being the wiser about me Donald Ducking it.

And if I was feeling horny, I could even manage to sneak a quick jerk-off session in between—or even during—those calls. Yeah, apparently divorce has made me naughty.

Hell, I was still a virile, healthy, red-blooded man. Even though I was well into my fifties, I still felt like I was twenty years younger. I was into sports all my life, wrestling since my teenage days and all through the college, and it showed. Okay, these days I was a little soft around the middle, but I was still in better shape than any of my 'dad bod' buddies. And by the secret (and not-so-secret) glances their wives threw my way, I'd say they noticed. A gay employee had recently informed me that I was what's called a 'silver fox,' which is just a nicer term for DILF—and everyone knows what that means.

Sometimes, though, the house felt barren with only me around. It seemed too big, hollow, silence stretching through the hallways and filling up the rooms like an invisible cobweb. My newfound solitude was still too fresh to be gloomy or oppresive, but I wondered how long it would take until freedom turns into loneliness.

That July morning I woke up too early—my bladder was not getting with the program and definitely felt my age, forcing me to get up during the night and pay a visit to the can. After I took a leak, I didn't feel sleepy anymore, so I put on a pair of flip-flops and went outside on my front porch to have a smoke. The dawn was breaking, washing away the darkness of the night, and the summer air was warm enough to feel pleasant on my naked skin.

I leaned on the porch railing and lit a cigarette, enjoying the feeling of being naked outside. I'm no exhibitionist or anything, but there was no one around this early, and it felt quite liberating being so… free. As I gazed into the sky, where the last stars were fading before the rising sun, my hand went to my balls, rolling them around my palm, then to my cock, which was starting to get a little fluffed. I tugged at it, feeling tingly all over, and it started to grow. Sighing deeply, I closed my eyes, surrendering to the sensations. I probably shouldn't, but… could I jerk it off right there?

There was something daring in it. A sense of liberty one rarely experiences living in the city. A feeling of unity with nature, with the universe. What's more natural than a man spilling his seed out in the open?

That's when I heard a voice nearby: "Good morning, Mr. Davidson."

Eyes snapping open, I saw Daniel, the neighbor's kid, standing in the driveway only twenty feet away. "Hello," I said trying to sound casual and putting my hand over my semi-hard cock in a vain attempt at modesty. I forgot that he was back from college during the summer break. But what the fuck was he doing awake and outside this early?

"Um, I had to take out the trash," he said like he had read my mind, then proceeded to dump two plastic bags into the garbage bin we shared on the driveway between our two houses. But instead of turning away and going back to his house, he then simply stood there, smiling sheepishly at me.

"Isn't it a bit early for that?" I said, not knowing what else to say.

"The garbage truck comes every morning at five-thirty," he said. "I forgot to do it last night, and had to set the alarm to wake me up, so Mom wouldn't be angry."

I nodded, smoking in silence, thinking this would be the end of our conversation, and he'll go back inside his house. But instead of going away, he stepped closer.

"Matt and Tyler are not here?" he said as he approached.

"They're in Providence with their mother this month," I said. "They'll come here in August."

"Oh. Right. Okay." He stopped only six feet away from me.

I noticed that his eyes were glued to my cock, still somewhat hidden behind my hand. I was used to getting stares at my junk all my life; most men are curious, especially when they see a big one like mine, and, honestly, it never bothered me. It was a compliment, really. And the attention felt good, even if it was coming from other men. Or twenty-something possibly gay guys, as the case was here.

Oh, what the hell, I thought; we're both adults and if he's so desperate to see it, then let him have it. So I moved my hand out of the way and let my cock be on full display, framed between two vertical rails of my portico. It was still somewhat fuller than flaccid, but nowhere near hard.

His eyes went wide, and his smile followed suit. He was standing in front of my porch like a man in a trance, my cock at his eye level. Yep, the kid was definitely gay. And I didn't want to send the wrong message, so I put out my cigarette, scratched my beard, and said, "Well, I'm going back to bed now. See you around."

"Oh, yeah, right," he stuttered, now staring at my ass as I walked away. "Good ni—I mean, good… Have a good day, Mr. Davidson."

"Jeff," I said, closing the door behind me with a wry smile. "You've seen me in my birthday suit so you might as well just call me Jeff."

And with a wink at the twink, I went inside to make myself a cup of coffee.

It was no use going back to bed, so I put on a tank top, shirtcocking like usual, and decided to start my work early. I had been working on a big construction project for the past two weeks, and I needed to confirm my design with the client before proceeding further. But by the time I finished with everything I had to do, I felt too tired even to fix myself something to eat. So I ordered a pizza and threw myself on the couch for a quick nap until my food arrived.

2

DANNY

Oh my God, I can't believe what just happened. I saw my hot-as-hell neighbor buck naked outside! Balls hanging, cock swinging, he was smoking a cigarette on his front porch without a care in the world. Wow.

I mean, I'd seen his package before—I used to spy on him as a kid, hoping to catch a glimpse of that huge cock sticking out of his shorts, and my diligence had been rewarded a few times. But never like this, never completely in the buff. And it was everything I ever dreamed of and more.

Jeff had always been a very handsome, very masculine hunk of a man. His family had lived next to mine for as long as I could remember. But the years had not lessened his hotness; age had only seemed to refine it. His hair and beard were more gray now, yet his body still looked the same. Those wide shoulders, those huge hairy pecs, those strong arms, and tree-thick legs… And that fat, uncut cock! Damn, did it look delicious. His ass too, round and firm like a rugby player's, peppered with soft fuzz like the rest of his body. Even his slight beer belly was fucking hot, giving him a sense of 'realness' that all those gym bunnies never managed to possess. He was a true man's man, big, bearded, and burly, a furry beefcake still in his prime. If I wasn't gay before, the sight of him naked would've turned me for sure. In fact, he was the reason that I realized I liked men in the first place. My first crush. My first sexual fantasy.

Of course I had to jerk off now, after seeing him like that.

But one nut wasn't enough, and I kept thinking about him throughout the day, getting hard and touching myself, wondering what he was up to. I wanted to see him again, talk to him again, and I desperately searched for an excuse to visit him. Then it hit me: I still had a book I'd borrowed from his son Matt months ago—I could go over and return it! Yeah, it was kind of obvious, but I couldn't care less. I just wanted to be alone with him.

So I dug out the borrowed book and hopped over to his house. As I climbed the steps to his porch, the scene from this morning flashed before my eyes, and my cock twitched inside my shorts. Dear God, I was getting hard again from simply thinking about it. Taking a deep breath, I paused for a few seconds to get myself under control. When I felt I was ready to face him again, I finally knocked on the door.

No one answered. I knew he had to be inside, because his car was still in the driveway, and I was watching his house all day like a hawk, so I would've noticed him leaving. I knocked again, then again. Still nothing.

Having finally gathered my courage to confront him, I wasn't giving up that easily. After contemplating my next move for a few moments, I went around to his backyard, intending to call him and try my luck there. A bit invasive, I admit, but I was getting desperate. When I approached the back door of his house, I saw them being wide open, only the screen door keeping the bugs from flying inside.

And then I saw the scene in his living room.

My heart almost stopped beating right there. Because there he was, asleep, sprawled over the sofa with nothing on but a black tank top and a pair of black low-cut socks, his lower body naked and exposed. Legs spread wide, hands behind his head, his fat cock resting on his thigh, his massive ballsack on full display—he was a sexual fantasy made flesh.

Should I go away now? But... But I had already seen him naked and he wasn't bothered.

So I guess he wouldn't mind me coming inside, would he?

"Um, Mr. Davidson?" I mumbled. "J-Jeff?"

He must have been very tired, or a super sound sleeper, because he didn't even stir. So I opened the screen door and let myself in, stepping into the large living room. I tiptoed to the couch he was sleeping on, soaking in the view. God, he was perfect, so muscular and *thick.* I didn't know where to look first, at his hairy armpits, his spread legs, or the main prize at their center. I didn't think I'd ever seen balls that full and huge in my entire life—and I'd been with plenty of hung guys before. And his cock, fatter and longer soft than most men's when erect.

I knew it was wrong, but I couldn't stop myself—I had to touch him. I reached out and fondled his smooth nutsack, obviously freshly shaved, rolling those gigantic nuts in my hand. They were so warm and heavy that my mouth watered. Then I touched his cock, stroking it slowly, and it started to grow under my ministrations, reaching its full size in a matter of seconds. Jesus, what a monster it was! A solid nine inches in length and at least eight in circumference—I couldn't even close my fist around it; how could anyone fit that into their mouth?

"Mmmmph," he groaned in his sleep and his cock twitched in my hand.

Before I knew it, I was sucking him. I licked the tip at first, my tongue collecting a pearly drop that oozed from the slit. Then I started to suck on the engorged head like it was a lollipop. I heard him moan somewhere above me and wondered how I would explain this when he woke up. But whatever may come next, I knew I had to use this chance. So I opened my mouth as wide as I could and swallowed as much of his cock as I could.

I felt it hit the back of my throat, and it was only halfway inside my mouth. I relaxed my jaw and pressed on. Inch by inch, it slid past my uvula and down into the depths of my upper esophagus. Tears streamed down my cheeks. I couldn't breathe, but I didn't care; I had him, all of him, in my mouth!

All of a sudden, I felt his hand on my head, holding me in place, as his hips began to move and he started to fuck my face. With every thrust, it seemed his cock pushed deeper, choking me, and my gag reflex almost made me throw up. He used my mouth like a fucktoy, without mercy or regard for anything but his own pleasure. The spit was drooling down my chin, the tears were flowing, and my throat was burning, but I never wanted it to stop.

As I wondered how much of this sweet torture I could endure before I actually suffocate, I felt the familiar spasms and pulsating of his cock. Hot cum erupted from it and into my gullet. I couldn't taste it because he was buried so deep inside my throat that it went straight to my stomach. But knowing that he'd come in my mouth made me come too, leaving a mess inside my shorts.

I pulled back enough so I could breathe again, but I didn't let his cock slip out of my mouth yet. I continued to lick and suck on it as it softened. Still reluctant to relinquish my prize, I looked up at him just as he opened his eyes. As the realization of what had happened hit him, shock spread across his face.

"What the fuck—?"

3

JEFF

THE BLISSFUL WARMTH unfurled over my body as I felt those familiar feelings of getting a truly great blowjob. In my dream, some busty blonde was giving me head as I lounged in my bed. In reality, I was never much impressed with oral sex, because none of my girlfriends could take my cock all the way in. But the blonde vixen deepthroated me like a pro, finally fulfilling a lifelong fantasy. Soon, I came down her throat so strong I shuddered like I was being electrocuted.

Wow, that was some blowjob!

But something felt off. It was too real to be a dream. And it should have been over now that I'd come, but I could still feel soft lips wrapped around my meat, licking it clean. So I brushed off the lusty visions and opened my eyes. And I saw the neighbor's kid, Danny, crouching between my legs and sucking my cock.

"What the fuck—?" I yelled. I almost fell off the couch as I jumped, pushing him away.

"Mr. Dav—Jeff," he said, red in the face. "I am so sorry! I came to… to return the book Matt lent me, and I… I saw you sleeping, and… and…" He buried his face in his hands, still on his knees. "Oh my God, I am going to die."

"Daniel," I said, standing over him, hands on my hips, struggling to find the right words. My semi-hard cock was still wet and dripping from his saliva, kind of ruining the serious mood I was going for. "That was not okay. I was asleep and not aware of what was going on… I didn't realize it was you! I would've never allowed that to happen otherwise!"

"Please don't tell my parents," the kid pleaded, rising up.

Well, that would be an awkward conversation to have. How would I even explain it? "I won't tell anyone," I said, and he relaxed a little. "But you should go home now. And don't even think of doing that again."

But as I said it, some depraved part of my brain rebelled, thinking: *Are you sure about that? The kid just gave you the best blowjob of your life. The first and only time someone has managed to take your entire cock in and deep-throat you. And you want to throw it away, just like that?*

I'm not gay! My conscience shouted, but that wicked part didn't want to give up: *A mouth is a mouth. What's the big deal?*

I looked at him; the kid was on the verge of tears. I couldn't send him home like that. "Look—" I began, but then the bell rang. So I stomped across the room and jerked the door open. A delivery guy stood on my porch, holding out my pizza. I paid him, said thanks, and shut the door behind him, bringing the pizza box to the living room, where Danny stood looking at me wide-eyed like I was some sort of alien. "What?" I said, placing the box on the table, still a little annoyed.

"You… You went and opened the door like that…" He was gesturing at me, and I remembered I was still naked from the waist down, Porky Piggin' it, cock all shiny from his spittle. So that's why the pizza guy was smirking. The funniest thing was, Danny looked at me with open admiration in his eyes. He was in awe.

"Okay, look…" I said. Then I opened the pizza box and pushed it toward him, the aroma of melted cheese and tomato sauce making my stomach growl. "Have a slice, and we'll talk things through." He sat down and I brought two plates from the kitchen, then went to the fridge, picking a Bud Light for me and a Coke for him.

"I'm twenty-three, you know," he said as I placed the can on the living room table next to his plate. "I could drink beer too." But he took the soda and gulped it down.

I sat in an armchair opposite him, and for a time we simply ate in silence. Whenever I looked at him, he was staring at my crotch. When he noticed I was watching him, he lowered his gaze, embarrassed that I had caught him. But after a few moments, he started staring again, like he was unable to help himself. And it didn't escape me that my horny little neighbor was sporting a visible tent in his shorts, which were already wet in the middle. Oh boy. I thought I should go and put some shorts on, but I guessed it was kind of late for that, anyway.

"What you did was wrong," I finally said to him, sternly but in a calm voice. "I didn't give you permission, and you used me." As he started to apologize again, I put my hand up, cutting him off. "However—I'd be lying if I said I didn't enjoy it."

His face lit up like a Christmas tree. "You did?"

"Well… yes. But that doesn't mean it will happen again."

"Oh." He was crestfallen once more.

I mean, *could* it happen again? I thought about it. He clearly wanted it. I clearly enjoyed it. So, what was stopping us? Yeah, I wasn't attracted to guys and didn't have any desire to reciprocate, but if he just wanted to suck me off from time to time… I wasn't bothered by the fact that he was a guy as much as the fact that he was the neighbor's kid, who used to play with my sons growing up. But he was all grown up now, and…

"What would *you* want, Daniel?"

"To suck your cock," he replied at once. "Whenever you want."

"Just that?"

He blushed. "Well… I'd like you to fuck me too, if you want…"

"Son, I'm not gay. I don't fuck men."

"But a hole is a hole—"

"*Daniel.*"

"All right, then. Just blowjobs."

My traitorous cock twitched. I took a long sip of my beer, leaning back in my chair. "Come here."

Danny swiftly sank to his knees and crawled across the carpet, settling between my spread thighs. He looked at my cock with adoration, then into my eyes, expecting my next order. So he liked to be told what to do, eh?

"Lick my balls," I said, and he went straight to it before I even finished the sentence. He lapped at my nuts like they were the most delicious dessert, while I finished the last slice of pizza. My cock began to grow. Danny certainly knew what he was doing, sucking and swallowing my balls one by one, rolling them with his tongue inside his hot wet mouth as my cock started leaking. "I was asleep the first time, thinking it was all a dream. Now, I want to experience everything while I'm fully aware. You're going to suck my cock, and then I'm going to fuck your mouth until I shoot my load down your throat again. Nod if that sounds good. Yeah, that's a good boy. Now take this big dick into your mouth and work on it."

4

DANNY

I WAS IN HEAVEN.

I literally thought I had died and went to paradise—or some horny, pervy, lustful version of it. That's how wonderful my life was at the moment.

Jeff and I were lovers. Well, 'lovers' in the sense that I had been sucking him off every day (sometimes multiple times) for almost a month and he never even kissed me, but still. It was all good. It was worth it.

I sucked his cock as he reclined on the couch in his living room, watching TV; in the kitchen, under the table, while he was eating or working; in his marital bed, where he straddled my chest and thrust into my mouth with abandon; in the shower, after I washed him head to toe, exploring his beefy body with my hands and my lips. At first, he wanted my mouth only on his cock or his balls. But lately, he'd given me more freedom. I started sucking on his nipples, licking his hairy armpits, nibbling his firm, round butt cheeks—even sneaking a few licks at his asscrack.

He didn't want to admit it, but I knew he liked it when I did all those things, those small signs of adoration that felt amazing as much as they boosted his ego. His nipples were especially sensitive, so hard and protruding from his hairy chest, and he started pushing my head toward them on his own accord. Soon, everything below the neck was open for my oral examination, and I used it to the full extent, never even expecting him to return the favor.

The farthest he'd go during our naked romps was grabbing my head to better fuck my mouth. Sometimes, though, after he would come, he'd go sweet and mellow on me, and start to rub my shoulders or stroke my hair like a lover would. Of course, he would stop the second he would realize what he was doing. But I still cherished those moments of rare affection and intimacy.

Then again, he was getting kind of handsy with my ass lately—squeezing it, slapping it as I slurped his cock, even rubbing my hole once. I figured it was only a matter of time before he actually fingered me, and I did all I could to encourage him: wiggle my ass at his face while I sucked him, position myself so that he had access to it at all times, or even taking his hand and placing it down there when he was too far gone to fight me.

It all paid off one day when, as I bent over his lying body, blowing him in his bed, I felt his finger probing my hole. I moaned around the hard organ in my mouth and swallowed it all the way in, showing my appreciation. But after a few tentative strokes, the finger disappeared. My disappointment lasted only for a moment, because the next thing I knew, the finger returned, this time lubed with his spit, pushing into me.

It drove me abso-fucking-lutely wild. My whole body shivered as his finger worked its way inside me, and I went to town on his cock like I never did before. It pleased him, because I heard him hiss above me and his dick throbbed in my mouth like a goddamn vibrator.

"Yeah, you little slut," he said, almost growling. "Swallow that cock like the good little cock-sucker you are… Yeah, like that… Mmmm… Oh yeah… You like it when I play with your ass? Yeah? You want me to push deeper? Faster? Or how about…" Another digit joined the first one, and he began to finger-fuck my hole for real. Whenever he grazed my prostate, I thought

I'd faint from pleasure. I whined, which only made him hornier.

Unable to control myself any longer, I came without even touching my dick, and seeing it, he came too. Like always, I swallowed every last drop of his cum, and continued to slobber on his cock afterward, until it went soft in my mouth.

When I finally let it go, I pulled my shorts up, sat on my knees beside him, and appraised his naked body, satiated and sprawled over the sheets of his king-sized bed. He had a strange expression on his face, like he was studying me.

"So," he said. "You liked that? Me fingering your hole?"

"Yes!" I blurted out emphatically. "It's the best—except for having a real cock inside." This pushed him to contemplative silence, so I went on, playing on his curiosity. "I haven't been fucked in the ass for a very long time. I miss it so much. The feeling of a big, hard cock pushing into me and spreading my hole… God, it drives me wild just thinking about it."

He scratched his beard. "Huh. So gay guys really do enjoy that stuff?"

"Well, bottoms like me do. Or vers guys. But some are strictly tops and never take a cock up the ass. In the end, everyone gets exactly what they want."

"I can't even remember the last time I had anal. I think it was with one of my girlfriends before I met my ex-wife. She was the only one who let me fuck her in the ass—just once or twice. She didn't particularly like it, but she did it for me. Then we broke up, and…" He waved his hand. "Anyway. Guess women are wired a bit differently. Or maybe my cock's too big."

"It is big," I said, looking at his manhood resting on his stomach, "but even so, I'd love to ride it. I'd love to have it inside me, to have you pound me with it. When I jerk off in my room at night, I fantasize about it."

My words made his cock grow again like I knew they would. Even though I was aware that he wasn't attracted to me, he was at least intrigued by the idea of fucking my ass. After a month of constant blowjobs, his cock craved something new, something more. And here was the opportunity he might never find again. "Maybe…" he started. "Maybe, I don't know, we could try it?"

"Please, Daddy," I said looking at him, using my best impression of a lost puppy to stir his domineering side and goad him on. "Use me as you want. Put your big dick in my tight hole and fuck me hard."

My words worked like magic, and his cock rose to its full size, veins bulging, head glistening from precum. He took it in his hand and started playing with it, pulling the foreskin down and up, then stretching the string of precum from the tip with his finger. "Are you sure you can take it?"

"Yes," I said, breathless from desire. "I've been practicing with toys." I didn't mention that none of my butt plugs or dildos matched his size, but as long as we had plenty of lube and started slow, I was confident I could manage. Not wanting to seem presumptuous, I also didn't mention that I've been douching myself almost every day for the past week or so, hoping that his newfound interest in my ass will someday bear fruit.

He got up from the bed, his cock bouncing with every move, and nodded for me to take a doggy-style position. "Okay. Let's do it."

Bingo!

5

JEFF

IN TRUTH, I'm not sure what came over me. I guess it was true that a man can't use both heads at the same time, and I was clearly following the lead of the lower one, because I was about to have sex with a guy. The thought had never appealed to me before, never even crossed my mind, and if someone had told me I'd someday consider it, I would have laughed in their face.

And I'm not some closed-minded bigot or squeamish prude—I simply didn't find men attractive. I'd seen some gay porn and I hadn't been repulsed; I'd been bored, feeling nothing if there hadn't been a chick in the scene. There had been one drunken night in college, after a wrestling victory, when one of my buddies and I had shared a girl. I hadn't minded him being there or even brushing against him as our hands and legs had become entwined, but we had never *intentionally* touched or focused on each other. It had all been about teaming up to rail the girl sandwiched between us.

So, bearing all that in mind, I thought I'd have more reservations when the opportunity to have gay sex actually presented itself. I mean, sure, I was getting head from a guy this whole month; but then I could close my eyes and pretend, imagining whatever hot woman I wanted. Anal felt like I was about to cross the line— could I truly claim that I am one hundred percent straight after I do this? And yet, my dick was literally crying for me to stick it in this boy's ass, labels be damned. A mouth is a mouth; a hole is a hole; sex is sex.

Admittedly, Danny was a pretty boy—not quite effeminate but lean and smooth—and from behind, I could almost pretend he was a girl. Still, it was better not to dwell on that at all. Simply use his body, viewing him as an orifice for my cock—a necessary means to a pleasurable end.

He stripped his shorts and his T-shirt off and positioned himself on his hands and knees, while I rummaged through the drawer of my nightstand in search of lube and condoms. After finding everything I needed, I moved to kneel on the mattress behind him, putting on a rubber and looking at the offered hole that I was about to fuck. Head low on the pillow, ass sticking up, Danny was shameless in his desire for me, chanting all the while: "Yes, Daddy, come on and fuck me, please hurry up and put it inside, I want to feel it, I need it so bad…"

Who could possibly deny such a plea?

Needing no further prompt, I slathered the lube over his clenching hole and my throbbing cock, fingering him for a few moments before the penetration, to prepare him for what's to come. That's also something I didn't think I would enjoy but recently found out I was wrong. The feel of my fingers slipping inside his slick hole, the sight of them going in and out, drove me crazy with need to stick my dick inside.

And when three of my fingers sank into him without a hitch, I did just that: I aimed my cock at his entrance and started to push. I was met with immediate resistance, his asshole clenching in reflex. But as I kept pushing, applying more and more pressure, he relaxed, breathing deeply, and I felt the first breach while my cockhead slipped inside.

God *damn*. It was like a flaming vice was squeezing my cock, and it felt *so fucking good*. I thrust my hips instinctively, sinking deeper into him, and he yelped in pain. Yet he put his hand on my thigh, saying, "Don't stop. Keep going."

"Are you sure?" I asked, a little worried. "I don't want to hurt you."

"You won't. This is normal. My body needs time to adjust, that's all."

After that, I kept pushing, sliding slowly inch by inch, my cock becoming enveloped by a tight silky warmth I'd never felt before, until it was buried inside him balls-deep. And… wow. It was a sensation I almost forgot, yet even better, so much better than what I'd experienced in my youth, because here was a person who enjoyed it, enjoyed accepting my cock, who got off on it as much as I did.

"Oh, God, yes," Danny murmured in pure ecstasy. "So good… so big inside me… Oh yes… yes… I'm so full… God, I—I can feel it touching my second hole!"

I wanted to ask him what he meant by that, but speaking was difficult at the moment. But as I started to pull out and push back in, I felt the tip of my cock brushing on something deep inside his rectum, a muscle at the end of his colon that needed to open up the same way his asshole did. *A second hole!*

"Fuck me, Daddy," Danny moaned, delirious. "Fuck me hard!"

That's when I started pumping. Picking up the tempo with every thrust, I pounded his ass in a steady, fast, relentless rhythm, the sounds of his moans and my balls slapping his ass growing ever louder. His hole was making obscene wet noises as my cock slid in and out of it. Squeezing and clenching around my meat, that heavenly tunnel milked it as deftly as a hand would. God, that feeling… it was divine. I couldn't believe what I had been missing my whole life—I didn't even know sex could feel so raw, so intense. Because, for the first time, I could fuck without holding back, letting myself loose, and allowing my cock to sink as deep as it could, hitting the places in Danny's body that even he didn't know were possible to hit.

Slick with sweat, I collapsed on top of him, crushing him beneath my weight. My hips kept thrusting, driving my cock into his tight hot ass hard and fast as a jackhammer.

The orgasm came quicker than I wanted, heart-racing, toe-curling, and I could see the stars exploding behind my closed eyes. Roaring like a wild animal, I fucked him so roughly that the entire bed shook, on the verge of breaking apart, headboard banging against the wall as loudly as the boy that screamed under me.

It took me a few moments to recover and regain what little of my senses had remained. I kept lying on top of him, panting like a dog in the sun. Then the realization of what had happened hit me, and I sprang up, pulling out of him.

The boy lay motionless, save for the small sobs that shook his mauled body. His hole was wrecked, red, swollen, and gaping like a plundered cave.

"Danny?" I called out, throwing the used condom on the floor and pulling him up into my lap. He was boneless in my arms, unable to sit straight without my help, his face wet with tears. "Danny, I'm so, so sorry. I didn't mean to be so rough. Fucking you felt so good, I… I lost control. Are you in pain? Did I hurt you?"

He shook his head, wiping off his tears. "No," he said at last. "You didn't hurt me, Jeff. You made me cum so hard that I cried. I felt the orgasm not only in my dick but through my whole body… The pleasure was overwhelming. This was the best sex that I ever had in my entire life. These are the tears of joy."

And sure, there was a big wet spot at the center of the bed, where he had spilled his seed without even touching himself. I was glad that he was fine, but I was still a bit concerned. I swept the damp lock of hair from his forehead, took his face in my hands, and peered into his eyes. "Are you certain you're okay?"

"Yes," he said, sniveling but smiling at me. "I'm certain. Although I'm not sure I'll be able to walk—let alone sit—for a few days."

"Come on," I said, rising from the bed and pulling him up on his feet. He stumbled and leaned against me, clutching my shoulders for support. I held him safely in my arms, while he giggled like he was a little drunk. He looked almost high, staring at me like I was some god-damned hero, and I couldn't send him home like that. So I carried him to the bathroom shower and, turning on the warm water, I washed him head to toe, gently yet thoroughly, like he sometimes washed me.

6

DANNY

AFTER THAT FIRST TIME, Jeff couldn't get enough of my ass. He wanted to fuck me every chance he got, although we had to wait for a few days after the first time, because my hole was too sore to withstand another such assault. Even my parents noticed I was walking funny and winced whenever I sat down, so I had to make up some lame excuse about hurting my back in the gym.

"What's with the sudden interest in working out?" my Dad remarked, being that 'going to the gym' was my alibi for all the time I spent at

Jeff's. If I didn't start looking like The Rock soon, he'd get suspicious for real.

But I was too happy to care. I went back to sucking Jeff's cock the very next day, both of us biding our time until the main course was on the menu again. As soon as I felt sufficiently recovered, I told Jeff I was ready to be fucked again. He wanted to wait a few more days, considerate as he was, but I insisted—the look of pure lust in his eyes at the prospect of fucking my ass again was plain as day.

This time he was very gentle; after a lengthy fingering session, he fucked me slowly for almost an hour, crouching behind me, only picking up his pace at the very end. By the time he came, my ass was so accustomed to his cock that it felt like it was made to hold him inside, my sphincter stretched for him, my rectum reshaped to his cock's image. There was no pain anymore, no discomfort. Only the absolute, heavenly pleasure.

For the next two weeks, Jeff kept fucking me in every position he could think of: spread across the kitchen table, sideways on the couch in his living room, standing up and nailing me against the wall, soaped up in the shower, sitting in his armchair while I was riding him, lying on top of me in his bed—you name it, we did it. A single day couldn't pass without his cock shoved inside me, often more than once. His virility and stamina put even my own libido to shame. And the best of all, he didn't even need to hold back anymore; he could be as rough and wild as he wanted. In fact, the harder he fucked me, the more I loved it.

The only thing that would make it even more perfect would be if he bred me raw, but he insisted on using condoms. After commenting once that I missed his cum, since he always finished inside my ass these days, he compromised by pulling out before the climax, tossing the condom aside, shoving his cock in my mouth, and shooting his load down my throat like he used to in the beginning. I think he got off on the image of his cock going from my ass straight to my mouth, and that became the new standard afterward.

There was one other thing, though. It started bothering me a little that he always fucked me with his eyes closed. Usually, he preferred positions where we didn't face each other, but on those rare occasions when we did, I studied his flushed, sweat-covered face, loving the look of pure bliss on it. But he kept his eyes shut for as long as he could help it, determined to avoid the truth of whose hole he was fucking.

On the other hand, he started cuddling with me after sex instead of sending me home as soon as he came. We began spending more and more time together *not* fucking, simply cuddling on his couch in front of the TV, sharing meals, or lounging in his large bed wrapped in each others arms, just talking between our lovemaking sessions. It was so easy to talk to him; even though he was much older, he never once talked down on me or acted condescending. His maturity and experience gave him a warmth, empathy, and patience I'd never found in guys my age.

He asked about my time at Princeton, my plans for the future, my hobbies and stuff, showing an interest in me that honestly took me by surprise. He also opened up a little, sharing bits and pieces from his own life, which is how we discovered we had more in common than we thought—I was majoring in Architecture and Engineering, and he was running a successful Architectural firm here in Stamford. He even offered to set me up with some internship positions after I graduate.

Yeah, if it isn't obvious enough, I'm just gonna come out and say it: I was falling in love with Jeff. I'd been falling in love with him since the first moment I tasted his fat cock, but now I was completely head over heels. Rationally, I knew it could never be and he didn't feel the same way about me. But I quashed that thought, repressing the truth so as not to get depressed. I didn't want to spoil what we had, and if I confessed my feelings for him, it could mean the end of our little clandestine affair. And the thought of losing him scared me shitless.

I had no right nor reason to complain. I always knew what I was getting into, and the rules of our deal were simple—it was only sex; nothing more, nothing less. He already gave me more than what we'd originally bargained for, fucking me with more passion, diligence, and attention than any boyfriend I ever had. If I could ask for one more thing, that would be for him to kiss me; just once, to meld his lips with mine, to shove his tongue in my mouth and let me taste him that way.

Was it possible? Could it happen? We were already pushing the limits of our agreement, and despite being grateful, I was also becoming increasingly greedy. And it seemed that Jeff was opening up for more and more kinky stuff that he didn't think he'd like at first but was now curious to try. He truly shocked me one time when I felt his tongue on my hole. He was behind me, preparing me for his cock, when all of a sudden, his mouth replaced his fingers, and his tongue started lapping at the puckered flesh. My body shook in ecstasy as I whimpered for him to keep going, and he did, he rimmed me until I was close to cumming. Then he rammed his cock inside, hitting my prostate, and I came like a fucking geyser.

So I kept my hopes up, knowing that one of these days something had to give. And then it did. Just not the way I was imagining it.

It happened one sunny August afternoon, when Jeff fucked me on the couch in his living room. I was on my back, legs on his broad shoulders, while he pressed on top of me, his cock buried deep inside my hole, pistoning in and out. We were nearing the climax, lost in the heat of passion, blind to everything but the friction of our bodies. His eyes flew open, locking with mine, and he saw the look of joy and surrender on my face. I licked my lips, moaning his name. He lowered his face closer to mine, his hot breath on my cheeks, his beard tickling my chin, his lips almost brushing mine…

"Oh, for fuck's sake, Dad!" a voice behind us pierced through our daze. At that point, I was cumming so hard I could barely register it.

7

JEFF

THINGS BETWEEN DANNY and me recently took a strange, unexpected turn. As we spent more and more time together, we started bonding as friends, and it became harder to view him only as a fucktoy whose sole purpose was fulfilling my carnal needs. I wasn't blind; I could see that the kid had developed a crush on me, and it was partly my fault for keeping him around after sex and sending mixed signals. But even though I came to care for him as a person, I couldn't feel the same way about him, and I figured I should set the record straight. Pun intended.

Yet my resolve melted as soon as we started messing around. I admit, I was weak; it was enough to feel his mouth on my cock, or have my cock buried in his ass, to abandon all thoughts of establishing clear boundaries. In those moments, I would do anything he asked, anything to please him. He brought so much joy and pleasure into my life that I felt like I owed him more than I could ever repay.

There was also one other thing: I was afraid he would want to stop doing this if I rebuffed him. Yes, we always knew that this thing between us would eventually end. As soon as the summer break was over, he would go back to college and our fuck-fest will be done. But I was selfish and I wanted to keep doing it for as long as we could. After all, the problem will resolve itself when he leaves for Princeton. So I kept fucking him and said nothing.

That day, my dick was drilling his guts when I made the mistake of looking at his blissed-out face. It's something I always avoided doing before, so I could at least keep an illusion of distance, still not ready to face reality. But now something got the better of me, and I opened my eyes. He gazed at me so reverently, like I was a God, and the way he called out my name made my cock throb inside him. Who could've remained unaffected by such adoration, such open worship? The urge to kiss him overpowered me—a compulsion to taste those lips that so often enveloped my cock, to suck on that expert tongue. I wanted to try it. I always loved kissing, always felt it added to the pleasure, and I realized now how much I'd missed it.

So I lowered my head and went for it. But before our lips could touch, the sound of the door opening behind my back stopped me mid-motion, and then the voice of my older son drowned out Danny's moans.

"Oh, for fuck's sake, Dad!" Matt said.

"Jesus!" Tyler, my younger one, added the next moment.

I wish I could say that was enough to stop me. But feeling Danny's asshole contract and spasm around my cock triggered my own orgasm, and I kept pounding him until the last drop of cum was drained from my balls. And my two sons stood there frozen in shock and watched as I fucked him, balls slapping his ass, cock pumping in and out of a red, wet ring, all in Super Technicolor.

"Boys, go to your rooms!" I ordered as soon as I was able to think and speak again, but no sound came from behind my back, both of them still glued to the spot like they were turned to stone. Danny was staring at me like a deer in the headlights, still shielded from their view by my body, as mortified and frozen as they were. I pulled out of him, peeled off the cum-filled condom, and threw it away on the floor. Then I stood up, finally turning to face my scandalized sons.

I didn't have any clothes nearby to cover up, so I kept standing naked before them, hands across my chest, cock still half-hard and shiny from cum. They'd seen it all before and weren't fazed in the slightest. They were far more interested in the sight behind me, peering around to confirm what their eyes saw but their brains refused to process. Awkward, much?

"Daniel?" Tyler said, now more shocked than ever.

"What the actual fuck, Dad?!" Matt shouted, anger rising in his voice. "You're fucking guys now?"

"Mind your language, boy," I barked back, attempting to regain a shred of authority. "Daniel, pick up your clothes and go get dressed in the bathroom."

The poor kid jumped from the couch like it was lit on fire, grabbing his garments scattered across the floor with such speed that he resembled a moving blur. He ran to the bathroom and locked himself in. Speaking of which…

"I thought the door was locked?" I spoke calmer.

"They were," Tyler said, speaking as if in a trance. "We have the key."

"Right. Well, next time ring the bell. If the doors are locked, they are locked for a reason."

"I can't believe this," Matt said, still outraged. "First Mom, then my brother, and now you!"

I was moving around the room in search of some discarded pair of shorts—I could have sworn I had them around here somewhere—but this stopped me in my tracks. "What are you talking about?"

"Nothing," Tyler cut in, elbowing Matt.

"Well, you said you wanted to tell him," Matt replied, looking at him. "Might as well do it now."

"Tell me what?" I asked.

"I'm—" Tyler began, then stopped. His mouth worked in silence for a few moments, then Matt sighed and said:

"He's gay."

"I'm gay," Tyler confirmed. "At least… I think so."

"Guess I'm the only normal one around here," Matt said bitterly.

"Matthew, apologize to your brother right now!" I yelled, suddenly bursting with rage. "Being gay is perfectly normal, and I'm very disappointed in you for thinking like that. Is that the way I raised you?"

Matt looked truly abashed, and my anger vanished as quickly as it came. "I'm sorry," he said, eyes fixed on the floor, his words aimed at no one in particular, but meant for both Tyler and myself. "I didn't mean it like that. You know it," he added, shoving Tyler lightly.

Tyler nodded, shoving him back, and I knew that, when the dust settles, we'd be fine.

"Okay," I said. "Why don't you go to your rooms and unpack while I put some clothes on. Then we'll have something to eat and we'll talk about whatever you want to talk about. Deal?"

"Yeah, I think we saw enough of your junk for the time being," Matt said as he turned to go, a smirk playing on his lips. Now that the shock and confusion had begun to wear off, he was more like his usual wry self. Tyler chuckled and followed him upstairs, leaving me alone in the silent living room.

I strode to the bathroom and knocked on the door. "Danny? Everything okay in there?"

Danny opened the door looking at me like a trapped wild animal.

"Don't worry, I'll sort things out with my kids," I tried to reassure him. "But it's best if you go home now."

"Right," he said, emerging from the toilet. "Um, here," he added, offering me a pair of mesh basketball shorts. "They're yours. I grabbed them by mistake."

"Thanks," I said and put the shorts on, finally making myself decent. We stared at each other for a few beats, feeling like we should say something, but not knowing what. Since no words came, I walked him to the front door and bid him an awkward goodbye. I didn't yet realize just how final that goodbye would be.

8

DANNY

J EFF REFUSED TO SEE me while his sons were staying at home, saying we should pause our trysts as long as they were around, and a week flew by. A long, sad, empty week of hollow jerking off, without the taste and smell and feel of Jeff's big cock. By the end of it, August was already over and it was time for me to return to college for my final year.

I went to Jeff's house one more time before I left town, just to see him again, but it was Matt who opened the door and said his dad was busy. It was plain as day that Matt didn't like the idea of his father fucking a guy his age—especially one he used to play with as a kid. I tried pleading with him, asking him to let me in, but it was useless. I couldn't shout or make a scene because my parents were still unaware of what was going on right under their noses. Although they started to suspect something was off, seeing how miserable I was all of a sudden.

"No more going to the gym, huh?" my dad observed one time.

It seemed I had even started losing weight without Jeff's cum to sustain me. I tried telling myself to let it go and stop being clingy; our relationship was a temporary thing right from the very start. I had no claim on him; he had no real interest in me. So I went away without saying goodbye, rejected and brokenhearted, to start a new semester in hopes of forgetting him.

Maybe it was good that it ended when it did, I tried to console myself. Before I fell even more in love with him. Maybe this was for the best.

But as the seasons changed and months dragged by, I didn't think less often of Jeff; I thought of him *more*. I missed him every second of every day, my body feeble without his cock, like a phone missing its charger. I buried myself in my studies, thinking that if I kept my mind busy, I'd stop obsessing over him. I even tried dating other guys, scouring Grindr and Tinder for any half-decent man, but no one truly interested me, no one could compare to him. So when December came, and I packed to go back home for the Christmas holidays, all I could think about was seeing Jeff again.

Pathetic, I know. But love makes fools of us all or whatever, as the saying goes.

When I finally got back home, itching all over from the need for him, my parents were taken aback by how pale and skinny I looked. Concerned about my health, they started asking questions, searching for the reason why I resembled a malnourished vampire. But no matter how much I wanted to, I couldn't tell them the truth, now… could I? My folks were always supportive of me, but I don't think they would understand this. There was only one thing that could make me feel better, only one cure in the world: Jeff. And not only his cock, magnificent as it was. I wanted all of him. But I would accept anything he was willing to give me, however little that may be. It was still better than nothing, better than not having him in my life at all.

That first evening at home I was gathering my courage, biding my time, and waiting for my chance. Mom and Dad were fussing over me like I was a baby, so there wasn't a convenient opportunity to sneak out to Jeff's place anyway. Later that night, after we had a nice family dinner and my parents went to bed, I sat by the window in my room like a lovesick fool, looking at Jeff's house and watching the snow fall. It was turning the world pristine, covering the roof-tops with a soft white blanket. I thought about what I was going to say to Jeff when I see him, imagining us kissing, embracing, and fucking until fatigue finally dragged me off into the dreamland.

The next morning I woke up very early, too jittery to sleep. My parents were still slumbering, and realized it was now or never. Putting on my sweatpants and a hoodie as fast as I could, I tiptoed downstairs and wrapped myself in a warm winter jacket. I snuck out like a thief and ran to Jeff's house, leaving telltale footsteps in the fresh snow.

As I climbed to his porch where I first saw him naked, smoking a cigarette in the first light of dawn, the scene of that fateful encounter replayed in my mind. He was so confident, so sexy standing right there in the buff, that I felt lightheaded, weak at the knees. I knew even then that he was the perfect man for me, but I didn't dare hope he would ever return even a fraction of my interest in him.

Now, hope was all I had. Heart thundering in my chest, breaths turning into mist, I knocked at his door. A wreath was hanging there, a symbol of festivity. I might have been too old for Santa, but I still made a wish. Christmas was a time for miracles, right?

After a moment that seemed endless, Jeff opened the door. Wrapped in a fluffy gray bathrobe, scruffy and sexy as ever, he stood there, framed in the winter morning light. Staring at me.

9

JEFF

THE END OF MY RELATIONSHIP with Danny —and I could finally call it that—came more abruptly than I'd planned. But at the time, it seemed like the cleanest way to break things off, so I didn't fight it. What would be the point, anyway? He was supposed to leave town at the end of the week in any case, so why drag out the inevitable? That's why I busied myself with my sons, spending all my free time with them so my brain wouldn't go back to the lusty images of my cock being sucked by a slutty boy next door, or fucking said boy's sweet ass.

It was when Matt and Tyler went back to college that the real problem began. With the house all to myself again, I was left with the memories of all the things Danny and I had done in it, replaying all the hot sex we'd had everywhere, and I feared my cock might explode like a firecracker. I was whacking off more than I did when I was a teenager, but my hand was not enough. Nothing was. I was so horny I thought I was going mad.

Lonely and desperate, I let one of my buddies set me up with his wife's friend—a hot divorcee named Pam—and we went on a date a few days later. She was an attractive woman in her late forties, with a teenage daughter and two cats, but somewhat of a bore. It didn't matter; she could've been dull as dishwater for all I cared. Since I hadn't had a pussy or a nice pair of tits in forever, I was so focused on the prospect of getting in bed with her that nothing else mattered.

Three dates later, the wait was finally over and I was crazy with the pent-up lust. I took Pam to my bed and attacked her breasts with such ferocity that I tore the buttons of her blouse. I squeezed those bouncy boobs in my hand, sucking at her nipples, my other hand already sneaking under her skirt and between her legs to pull down her panties. She was wet and warm down there, but quiet as a mouse, small and barely audible gasps the only sound escaping her lips. Wanting to loosen her up, I rubbed her clit with my finger, then slipped it inside her cunt, but the first thing that struck me was how different it was compared to Danny's tight hole.

("Yes, Daddy, come on and fuck me, please hurry up and put it inside me...")

Angered by that thought, I went down on her, eating her pussy like a starving man. Going even lower, I licked her asshole, which in turn evoked a series of small tremors in her body. When she was dripping wet from my saliva and her own juices, I straddled her and brought my cock to her face. She licked the tip a few times, then turned her head away in silence, letting me know in no uncertain terms that that was all I was going to get in the blowjob department.

Disappointed but still eager to proceed, I put on the condom, positioned myself on top of her, and guided my cock into her cunt with my hand. God, yes—finally. Yet something still didn't feel quite right. As I started pumping into her, she kept lying there, motionless, squirming only when I picked up the pace, her hands flying to my hips to keep me at bay.

(*Fuck me, Daddy! Fuck me hard!*)

Apologizing, I slowed down, taking care not to shove my cock all the way in. At that point, both of us were more frustrated than horny, and when I finally came it wasn't very satisfying, only a shadow of the mindblowing orgasms I used to take for granted. I'm pretty sure she didn't come at all.

"I liked this blouse," she said later, as she put on the ruined garment, clicking her tongue in annoyance when she couldn't button it up. I just lay there naked on the crumpled sheets, my face probably as dark as my thoughts.

"I'll buy you another," I offered, to no response.

After she finished getting dressed, she spoke again. "That thing you did when, you know, you licked me *there*... I didn't like that. I got too self-conscious and couldn't enjoy myself after that."

"What thing?" I asked, but she only shook her head and refused to explain. "You mean when I licked your asshole?"

"Don't be so crude!" she hissed, frowning. "*Yes*. That."

"Well, you could've fooled me," I said. "Cause it didn't seem like you didn't like it. Quite the opposite, in fact."

My bluntness seemed to offend her even further—or maybe she couldn't face the truth about her own desires. *At least I could relate to that*, I thought. "I don't think we should see each other again," she said, and that was that.

Spending Thanksgiving alone was a gloomy affair. Matt and Tyler had decided not to come home until the Christmas holidays, so I skipped the turkey and grabbed takeout from El Chilito. Munching tacos on the couch and watching *Rocky* was pretty much my idea of heaven, but this time, it only served to remind me how empty my life had become. More than once, I caught myself glancing at my neighbor's house, looking for any sign of Danny. But there was none. I guess he didn't come home either.

I could've gone on more dates, tried a few other flavors, but to what end? I've been with enough women to know that none of them could offer me the same thing Danny did. It was basic anatomy, but even that aside, women simply didn't enjoy the same things men did, and that was perfectly fine. Yet where does that leave me? Do I resign myself to uninspired sex for the rest of my life—or take the plunge and embrace the possibility of fucking guys? After everything that transpired this summer, I had to accept the fact that I was bisexual. No point in denying it, especially in the face of the recent evidence.

But here's the kicker: I still didn't find men sexually attractive. When I tried to picture hooking up with guys, imagining them slurping on my cock, or taking me up their ass, I couldn't even get hard. But if I thought about *Danny*—bingo. Instant erection. It was like my body had been rewired to respond only to his, and I didn't know how to undo it. Would I even want to?

Because it wasn't only the sex, however awesome and life-changing it was. It was all those things in between our porny interactions that made all the difference: all the talks, the jokes, the shared interests that I missed now as much as I missed the fucking. And knowing all that, what am I going to do? What *could* I do?

I was still wrestling with all these questions and doubts when, just two days before Christmas, I heard someone call out my name at the grocery store. "Jeffrey."

Turning around, I saw Philip, Danny's dad, scarf snug around his neck and glasses slightly foggy over his flushed, clean-shaven face. Instant guilt burned my cheeks (thank God for the beard). How could I look the man in the eye after all the things I'd done with his son? We had only seen each other in passing since Danny had left, waving to each other or saying hellos across the yard. This was the first time we stood close enough for a real conversation. "Phil… Hi."

We exchanged the usual pleasantries and went into small talk about the prices and the economy. But, pushing our respective carts side by side, I could see that something was bothering him. As we touched on the topic of the Christmas holidays, I mentioned that my sons were coming over tomorrow to spend the winter with me. He said that Danny was going to stay with them, too.

"How is Danny?" I asked trying to sound casual, and he leaped on the chance to broach the subject.

"Not good," he said, "and judging by your look, neither are you." When I tried to brush off his comment and feign ignorance, he just raised his hand to cut me off. "Please, Jeff. I don't know what exactly happened between the two of you, but I'm not an idiot. I saw him sneaking over to your house multiple times all through the summer, and your bedroom window looks directly over at my upstairs bathroom."

My mouth was hanging open for a while before I could speak again. "You… You *saw* us?"

"I'd seen more than I cared to," he replied, turning scarlet from the neck up. "But my son seemed happier than ever, so I didn't say anything, didn't want to interfere. I figured he would come clean with me and his mother once he felt comfortable enough. After all, you are both adults, and I had known you long enough to trust you wouldn't take advantage of him—"

"Never, Phil, believe me," I had to interject. "I would never have coerced him into anything against his will. I get that our age difference is too big for some people to accept, especially having kids his age myself. I—I'd tried to be level-headed and responsible, but… I was lonely, and I was weak. I have no excuse."

"I don't need your excuse, Jeff," he said, putting a hand on my shoulder as if to reassure me, his expression softening. I understood then how Danny turned out into such a great human being. "What I need from you is to sort things out with my son. If you don't really care for him, let him know so he can move on. And if you *do* care for him, well, then… be a man and own up to it."

Well, that was a slap in the face that I sorely needed. I nodded. "I'll speak to him, Phil. I promise." I just needed to figure out what I wanted to say to him, first.

He nodded too and moved his cart in another direction. "Take care, Jeff."

The following morning Matt and Tyler came home, and the day flew by with the three of us decorating the Christmas tree and making the rest of the house look equally festive. All the neighborhood houses had been decorated weeks ago, but I hadn't felt like doing it without the boys around. It was something we always did together as a family, and even though their mother wasn't here—she was on her honeymoon in the Bahamas—I wanted to keep the holiday spirit intact as much as I could.

In the evening, as we gobbled on junk food and watched *Die Hard* per our tradition, the first snow began to fall, transforming the landscape into a real winter wonderland. The boys were having fun and I didn't want to spoil it, but every now and again, thoughts of Danny intruded upon my mind. I needed to have a serious talk with them too, right after I saw where Danny and I stood.

Speaking of fresh relationships, it seemed Tyler had found himself a boyfriend. Every few seconds, his phone chimed with a new message, and he turned bashful under Matt's teasing grin, shoving his shoulder against Matt's to make him stop. Yeah, the boy had fallen hard. His flushed cheeks and the way he kept glancing at his phone spoke volumes, but I didn't press him. Tyler would open up to me when he felt ready; he always did. Until then, I was content to watch the spark of something new and exciting unfold for him. For now, we could just relax and enjoy some good old-fashioned guy time together. *Yippee Ki-Yay, motherfucker.*

By Christmas day, everything was white. I got up super early, had a shower, and made myself a cup of coffee, wrapping a thick bathrobe over my naked body. Since the boys were at home, I stopped walking around nude as much, although they made up for it with their own shameless displays. It seemed that we had finally reached an unspoken agreement that the nudity was natural and not something to be ashamed of, so they used it to the fullest extent, parading around the house in the buff as much as they could. Loving the sense of closeness, freedom, and camaraderie it brought us, I felt no inclination to reproach them.

Sipping my coffee at the kitchen island and scanning the headlines on my phone, I heard someone knock at the door. It was still early in the morning so I had no idea who could it be. I went and answered, then stopped dead in my tracks. Because there, on my porch, stood the one person I most wanted to see in the whole wide world.

10

DANNY

"Hi," I SAID, my throat suddenly dry as a parchment.

"Hi," he replied, as if stunned.

After not speaking to each other for so long, I should've probably had some speech prepared, or maybe started with something like, 'Hi, Jeff, how have you been? What's new?' It didn't happen. Instead, my eyes traveled across his handsome bearded face, over the hairy chest, partially exposed thanks to the robe he was wearing, finally centering on his crotch. There, right below the loosely tied belt, a big juicy bulge kept on growing the more I stared at it. And soon, a fat cockhead emerged through the fold of his bathrobe.

"Jeff." It was the only word I could utter. The only sound I recognized, as I fell to my knees before him, right there on his doorstep, opened up his robe, and swallowed his cock. My hand closed around his massive balls, the other one sneaking up his torso, caressing the silver fur. It was like someone had injected life back into my body, every cell filling with cosmic energy, electrifying me back into a state of hyper-alertness. And while his hard cock slid down my throat, the world became vibrant again and fell into its place.

"Danny!" he moaned my name like it was an answer to a secret prayer. Grabbing my head, he pulled me onto his massive dong until it was lodged so far down my neck that it seemed about to touch my heart. His hips started thrusting, as he began fucking my face in earnest. But the next moment, he was pushing me away. "No, not here! Get inside."

He pulled me up roughly, literally throwing me inside his house and slamming the door behind us. Then he started tearing the clothes off of me, my jacket and hoodie thrown on the floor right next to his discarded bathrobe. Drinking up his naked body with my hungry eyes, I barely managed to peel off my shoes when he grabbed me in his arms and half-dragged, half-carried me upstairs to his bedroom. My sweatpants disappeared somewhere along the stairway, and by the time we reached his bed, we were both naked except for our socks.

He threw me over the mattress on my stomach, burying his face in my ass, growling like a wild beast as he started rimming my hole, his beard tickling me while I chanted like a monk in ecstasy: "Oh God, oh God, oh God…" I was soon completely wet from his lapping tongue and the precum that started leaking from my cock. "Fuck me, Jeff, please, I can't hold on any-more!"

Almost howling with need, my bearish daddy flipped me over on my back, settling between my legs. I loved his strength and how easily he could manhandle me. His monster cock jutted out from his beefy body, thick and throbbing, already slathered with lube. He must've done it while he was eating my ass, wasting no time to get inside me as fast as humanly possible. His eyes dark with hunger, he aimed it at my hole. But just as he was about to push it inside, he jolted, looking at me in alarm. "I have no con-doms! Danny, I don't think I can stop myself now…"

"Don't stop, Jeff, please," I begged him, tur-ned on beyond reason. "Don't worry, I'm clean, I got tested three weeks ago, and I haven't been with anyone since. Just keep going and breed me raw! Please!"

Perhaps my words reassured him, or he would've done it regardless of what I said, seeing he was as turned on as I was. Nothing else mattered when I felt his cockhead breaching me, his shaft entering my body, and all I could do was moan, "Oh, God, yes," over and over again. My asshole clenched around his cock, recognizing it not as an intruder but as a familiar source of pleasure that was sorely missed, squeezing it in welcome, and he finally started to fuck me hard and fast as a demon from Hell.

"Yes, Daddy!" I cried out. "Breed me! Fill my hole with your cum!"

This seemed to spur him to go even harder, even rougher than before, pounding me with the force of a hurricane. And during all that, he never closed his eyes. He kept looking at me, his eyes boring into mine, lust mixed with tenderness in them. Then, catching me completely by surprise, he crashed his lips with mine, tongue slipping inside. He kissed me like he wanted to devour me. It was deep and wet and sloppy, our first kiss, stretching into eternity. It left me breathless.

I came, spilling my cum between us, all over both of our stomachs and chests. Feeling the warm wetness on his skin and the rhythmic spasms of my hole, he came too, deep inside my gut, flooding me with his seed as I always wanted him to. And all the while, his lips never left mine.

Somewhere in the distance, I was aware of the sound of a door being opened.

"Dad, what's with all the noi—" I recognized Matt's annoyed voice even though I couldn't see his (surely shocked) face from my current position under Jeff's big body. But right now, I was so high on pleasure that I didn't even care he could see me spread out and stuffed full of his father's cock. Again.

"God dammit, Matthew, will you ever learn to knock?" Jeff yelled, turning his head to look at his older son over his shoulder, but otherwise not moving from his position on top of me. "Get the hell out, *now!*"

"Okay, this one's on me," Matt chuckled, sounding amused, not angry. "Hell, if this is your idea of Christmas, I gotta be here for New Year's!" As he shut the door behind him, we could hear him shout to his brother: "Ty, they're at it again! Don't even try going in there!"

That was simply too much and the laughter burst out of me like an explosion. Jeff looked at me like I had gone insane, then joined in, laughing as frantically as myself. The bed shook under us, the vibrations making our bodies rub and move, still joined, slick with sweat and cum. The friction made his cock start to harden again inside me and I wiggled under him in encouragement. "You have to install a lock on that door ASAP," I said as our laughter subsided into giggles.

"Mmm. Some curtains, too," he mumbled, nibbling at my neck. "Your dad also caught an eyeful, apparently."

"*What?*" I almost leaped in the air, but Jeff's body kept me secured in place. "Oh my God! *Oh my God!*"

"Relax," he said, continuing to plant small kisses all along my neck and face. "He was okay with it. Mostly. But it would be best if we sat with your parents soon and had a serious talk. Especially if we plan on… you know… being together."

I was left speechless for some time after that. I knew what I'd heard, but I still couldn't quite believe it. He made a small motion with his hips, reminding me that he was still buried in my ass, which finally brought me out of my trance. "You mean," I began, but my voice broke. "You mean, you want us to be together for real? Like… like a couple?"

"I mean, only if you want to," he said, sounding a little insecure. *I* was making *him* insecure? "I know I'm old enough to be your father, and you'll probably meet some hot dude your own age someday and get over me—"

I grabbed his face in my hands and kissed him deep and long. I still couldn't get used to how easily he surrendered his lips to me, sucking on my tongue as eagerly as I always sucked his cock. It was almost surreal. "Never gonna happen," I said after the kiss left us both panting for breath. "I had a crush on you ever since I was in elementary school. Besides, I always preferred mature, *elderly* men."

"Hey! Who are you calling 'elderly,' young man? Do I need to spank you to teach you a lesson?" Since he couldn't carry out his threat in our current position, he just rolled his hips, his fully hard cock swirling inside my cum-filled tunnel, hitting my prostate in the process and making my eyes roll back into my head. Since I could only gasp, he smiled wickedly and added, "I'll take that as a *yes*."

I was hard as a rock again, too. The thought of him spanking my ass almost pushed me over the edge, and I grabbed his firm round buttocks and pulled him even more into me. His cock slid over my gland and hit the second hole, making me whimper like a total slut, which I was for him anyway. I loved the slick, creamy sensation of his cum stuffing my ass; it served as a lube for the second round. "So what now?" I asked after I regained the power of speech again. "Should we go dress ourselves and have that talk with our families? Before you change your mind."

"Fat chance of that happening," he said, planting a small kiss on my lips after each word. "I was a fool to let you go once. I won't make that mistake again." He pulled back just enough so he could stare into my eyes. "I wouldn't do this if I wasn't serious about you, Daniel. You are the best thing that happened to me in a long, long time. I think we could have a future together."

Hearing him say that made me happier than I ever thought a man could be, and I had to bite my lip to stop myself from crying. Images of our life together flew before my eyes: me finishing one more semester at Princeton, then coming back here for good; moving in with Jeff; starting an internship at his firm and working hard until one day we become partners, in business as in life… The world was full of wonderful possibilities.

"Besides, what about this?" he asked, moving his hips in a languid rhythm and slowly sliding his cock in and out of my ass. My wet hole made little slurping noises with each of his movements, drenched with his cum.

"We'll have all the time in the world for that," I said, teasing. Like I could honestly ever deny him my ass. Like I even wanted to.

"True. But I was thinking about staying in the present and all that. You don't want me to go in front of your parents in this state," and he thrust his hips to emphasize his point, shoving his cock so deep into me. "Do you?"

"N-not a chance," I managed to stutter, wrapping my legs around his waist. "That thing is mine and mine only."

He chuckled and kissed me again, starting to pound me with increasing urgency. Soon, he was pistoning in and out of me with a force that shook the bed, making it slam against the wall while his balls slapped against my ass, eliciting muffled noises from the other side that sounded a lot like cheering. As his cock inside me redefined the meaning of pleasure, I almost started laughing again, giddy with delight, thinking about how things turned out. It seemed I had gotten my Christmas miracle, after all. And it was everything I ever dreamed of—and more.

Falling for a straight guy is never a good idea—especially when he's your ruthless, married coach.

Wrestling is hard enough for Tyler without the distraction of Blake, the team's hard-ass new coach. Blake is infuriating, impossible to please, and, unfortunately, the hottest man Tyler has ever seen. Too bad he can't stand him.

For Blake, this job was supposed to be a fresh start. He's here to rebuild his life, not to be challenged by a cocky, insufferable athlete who pushes all his buttons. There's just something about Tyler that makes him lose all self-control.

They clash. They push. They swear they hate each other.

But hate has a way of igniting into something else, something neither of them is ready for. And once the line is crossed, walking away won't be so easy.

ABOUT THE AUTHOR

Sebastian Hayden Azanon is an author of steamy, emotionally intense M/M romances that ignite the senses and challenge conventions. He likes his smut extra spicy, filled with complex characters, hidden desires, and plenty of witty banter. When not immersed in worlds of seduction and intrigue, he can be found hiking, working up a sweat at the gym, or arguing with his cat about life, the universe and everything.

ALSO BY S.H. AZANON

Stand-alone stories

Sweeter Than Sugar
In the House of Lilacs
The Palace of Lust
Windows
Epic Shores
The Black King of the Djinn

Straight Men series

The Neighbor *(Jeff & Danny)*
The Coach *(Tyler & Blake)*
The Boss *(Chris & Zac)*